Oxford University Press, Walton Street, Oxford OX2 6DP
Oxford New York Toronto
Delhi Bombay Calcutta Madras Karachi
Petaling Jaya Singapore Hong Kong Tokyo
Nairobi Dar es Salaam Cape Town
Melbourne Auckland

and associated companies in
Berlin Ibadan

Oxford is a trade mark of Oxford University Press

Text © John Bush 1991

Illustrations © Korky Paul 1991

First published 1991
First published in paperback 1992
Reprinted 1992
ISBN 0 19 279890 1 hardback
ISBN 0 19 272240 9 paperback

A CIP catalogue record for this book is available
from the British Library

Printed in Hong Kong

THE FISH
who could wish

JOHN BUSH & KORKY PAUL

For Carl and Kerri-Leigh JB
For the Tzannes family KP

Oxford University Press
Oxford Toronto Melbourne

In the deep blue sea,
In the deep of the blue,
Swam a fish who could wish,
And each wish would come true.
Oh the fun that he had!
Oh the things he would do!
Just wishing away
In the deep water blue.

He wished for a castle.

He wished for a car.

He wished for a horse
And a Spanish guitar.

Once, when he wished
He could go out and ski
It snowed for a week
Under the sea.

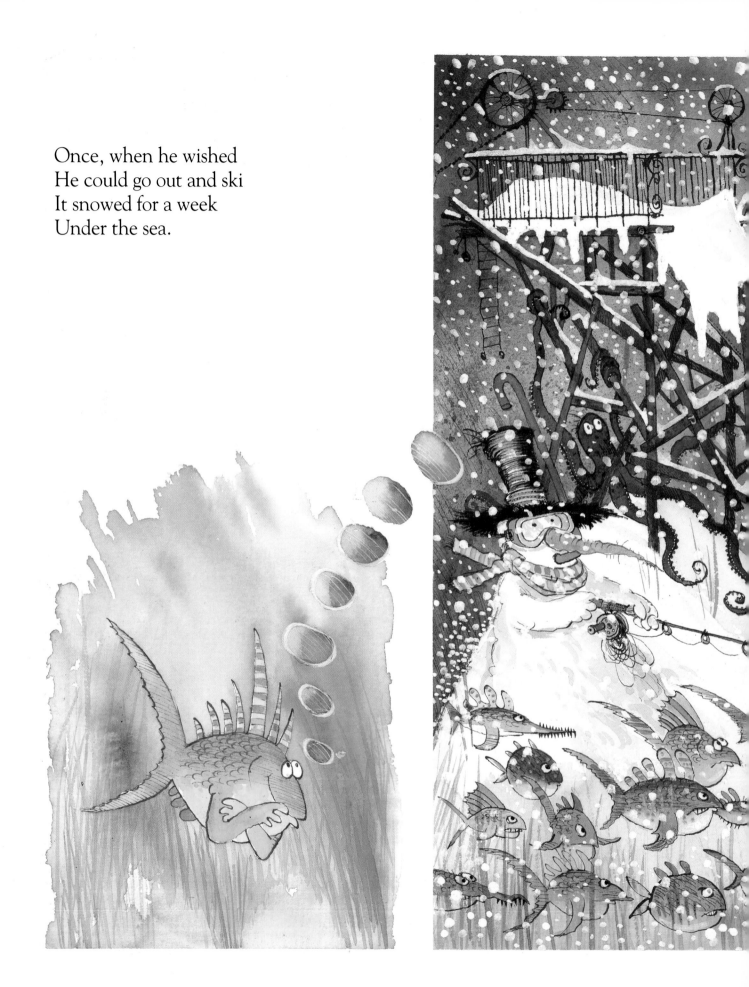

He wished he could fly
And to his delight,
Flew twice round the world
In exactly one night!

If sharks came a-hunting
For a nice fishy treat,
He'd quickly just wish
He was too small to eat.

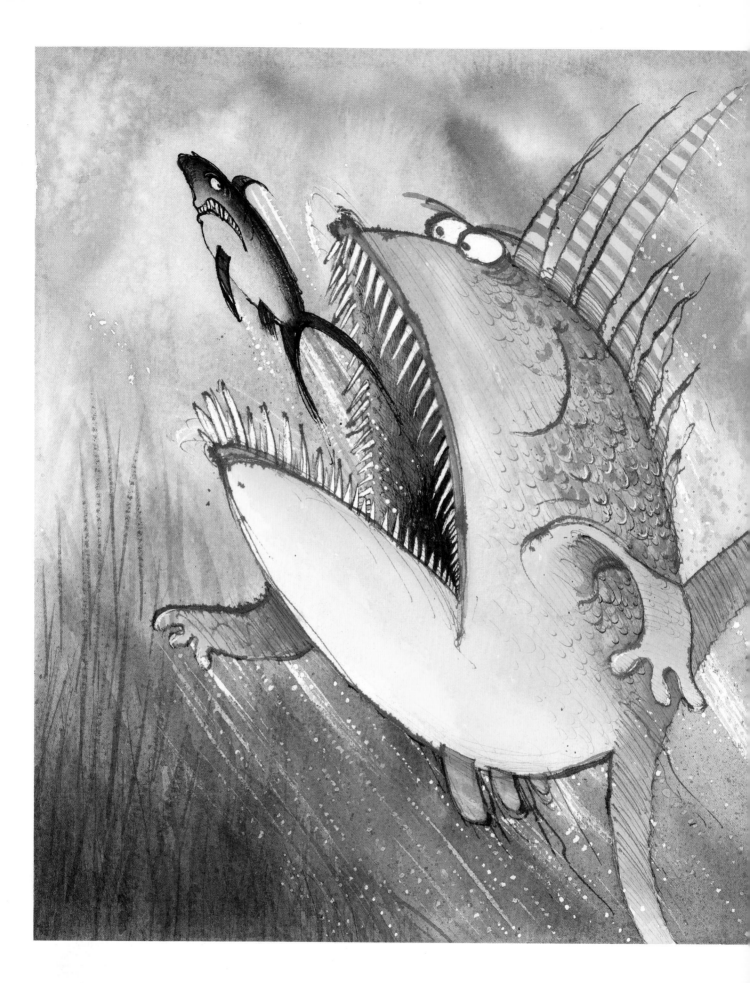

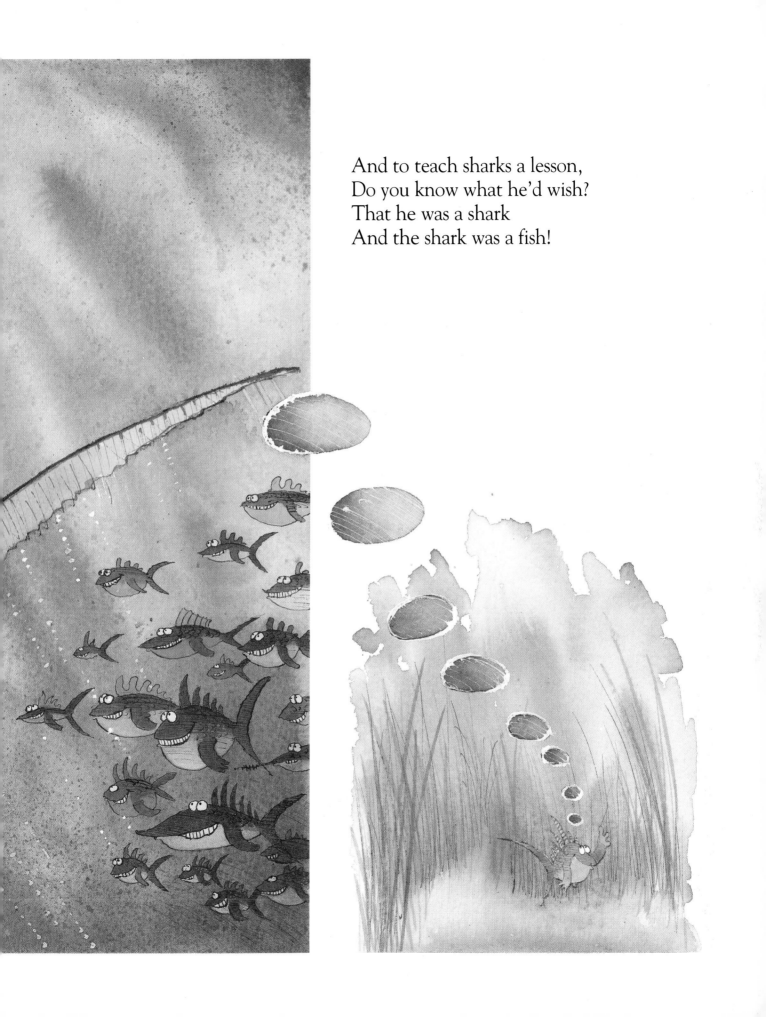

And to teach sharks a lesson,
Do you know what he'd wish?
That he was a shark
And the shark was a fish!

He'd wish himself square,
Or round as a biscuit,
Triangular, oval . . .
Name it, he wished it.

He wished for fine suits
And handsome silk ties,
But the one thing he never wished
Was to be wise . . .

One day, just for fun,
That silly old fish
Wished the silliest, silliest
Wish he could wish.

That silly old fish
Wished he could be
Just like all the other
Fish in the sea.
But wishing was something
Other fish could not do.
So that was his very last
wish that came true.